D1369562

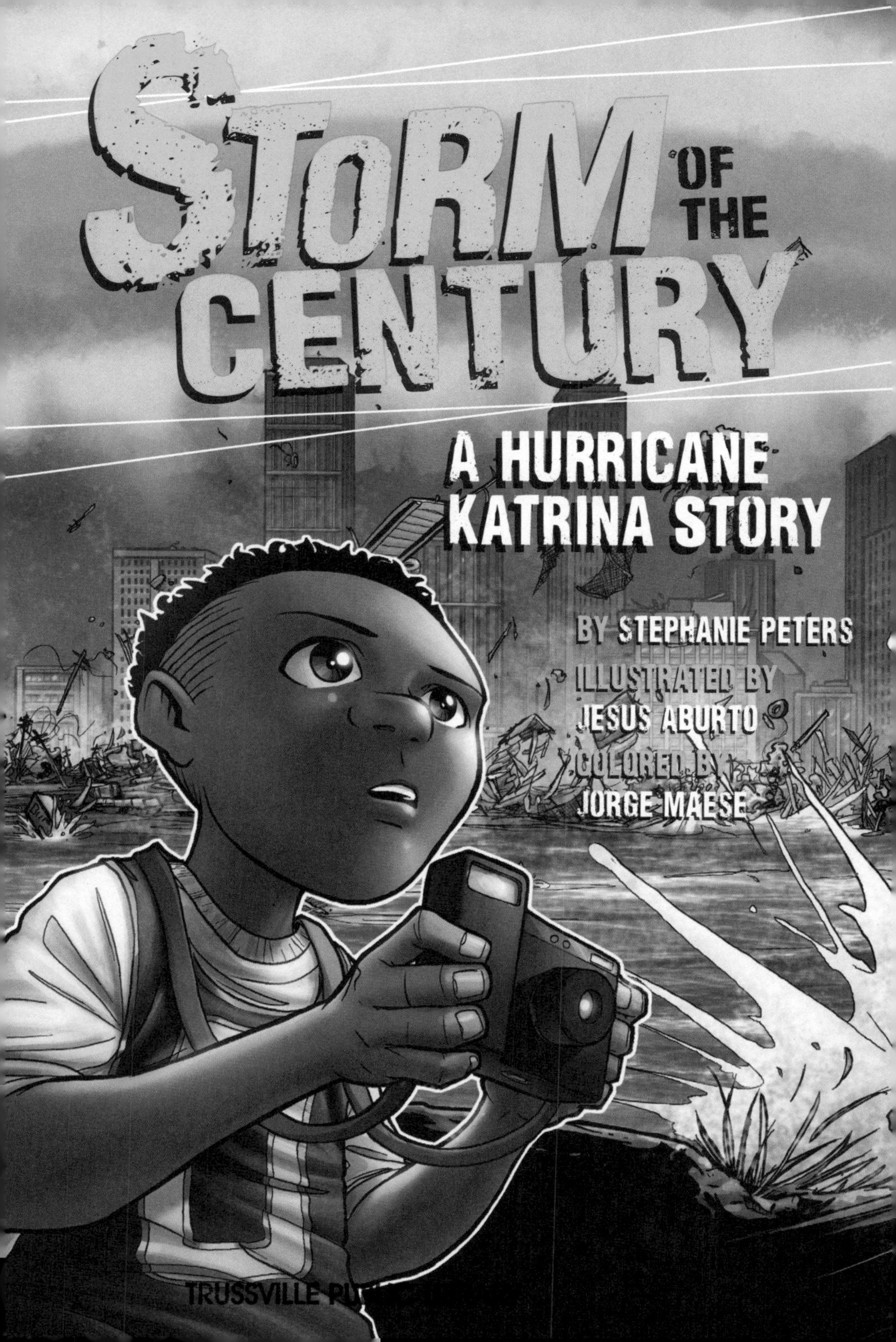
STORM OF THE CENTURY
A HURRICANE KATRINA STORY
BY STEPHANIE PETERS
ILLUSTRATED BY
JESUS ABURTO
COLORED BY
JORGE MAESE

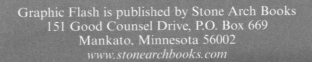

Graphic Flash is published by Stone Arch Books
151 Good Counsel Drive, P.O. Box 669
Mankato, Minnesota 56002
www.stonearchbooks.com

Copyright © 2009 by Stone Arch Books

Library of Congress Cataloging-in-Publication Data
Peters, Stephanie True, 1965–
    Storm of the Century: A Hurricane Katrina Story / by Stephanie Peters ;
illustrated by Jesus Aburto.
    p. cm. — (Graphic Flash)
    ISBN 978-1-4342-1164-4 (library binding)
    ISBN 978-1-4342-1379-2 (pbk.)
    1. Hurricane Katrina, 2005—Juvenile fiction. [1. Hurricane Katrina,
2005—Fiction. 2. New Orleans (La.)—Fiction.] I. Aburto, Jesus, ill. II. Title.
PZ7.P441833St 2009
[Fic]—dc22   2008032071

Summary: When Hurricane Katrina threatens New Orleans, Louisiana, 14-year-old
Ricky Thompson and his family must flee the city. Unfortunately, traffic is backed up
for miles, and there's no way out. As a last resort, the family takes shelter inside the
Superdome, a football stadium turned into a rescue shelter for thousands of residents.

Creative Director: Heather Kindseth
Graphic Designer: Brann Garvey

TABLE OF CONTENTS

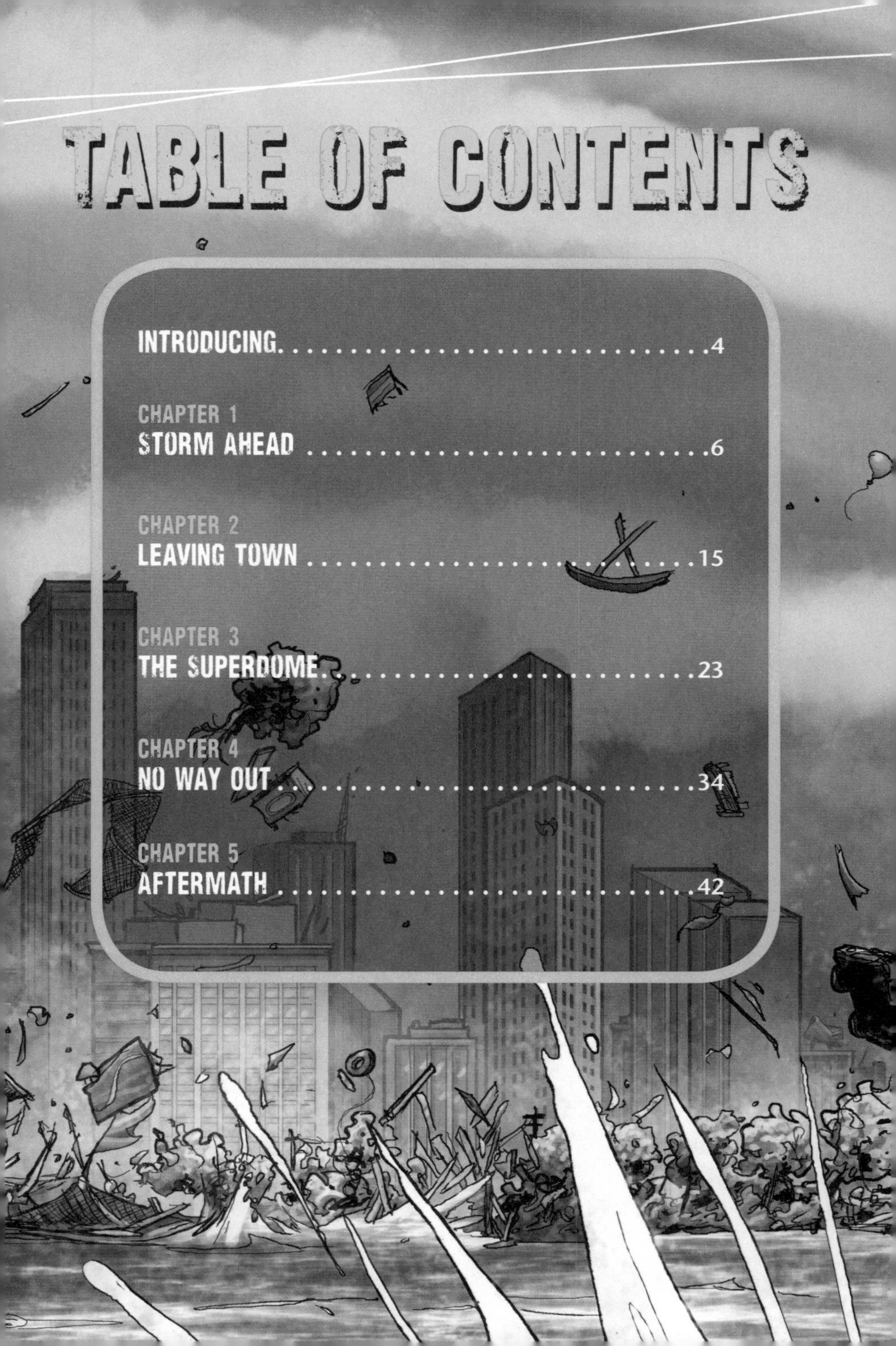

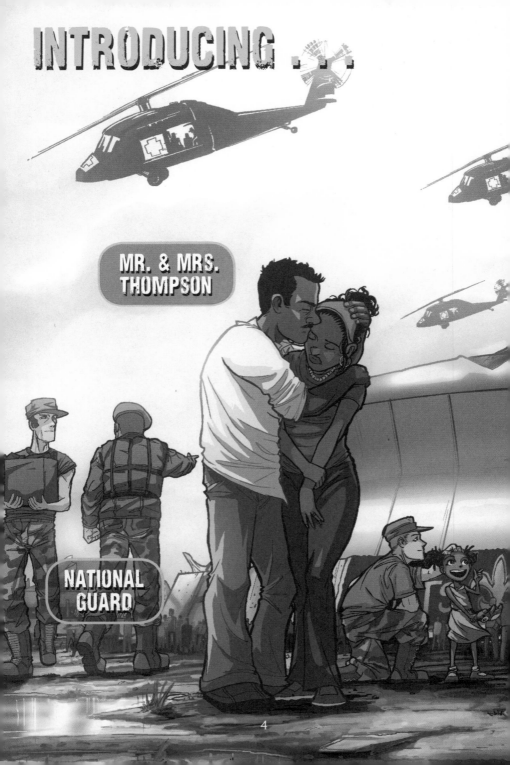

INTRODUCING . . .

MR. & MRS. THOMPSON

NATIONAL GUARD

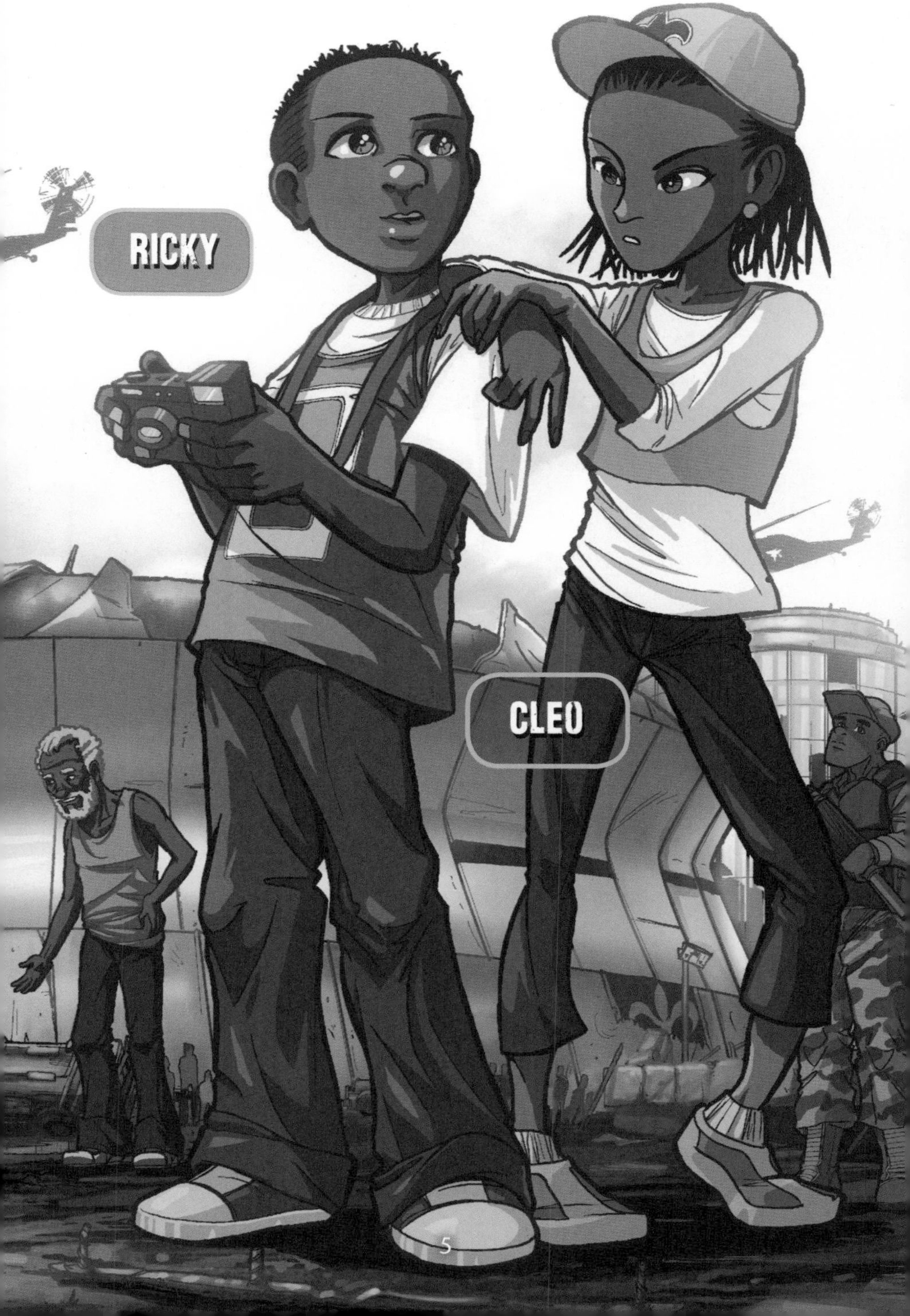
RICKY
CLEO

CHAPTER 1

STORM AHEAD

A thunderous banging echoed throughout the Louisiana Superdome. Thousands of people inside looked up in alarm. They watched in horror as one section of the dome above their heads, and then another, tore free.

Drenching rain poured through the gaping holes and onto the people standing below. Powerful winds howled over the openings, as Hurricane Katrina roared overhead.

Ricky Thompson was one of the people inside the Superdome. From his seat in the stands, he could see the huge tears. He quickly pulled out his new digital camera in awe.

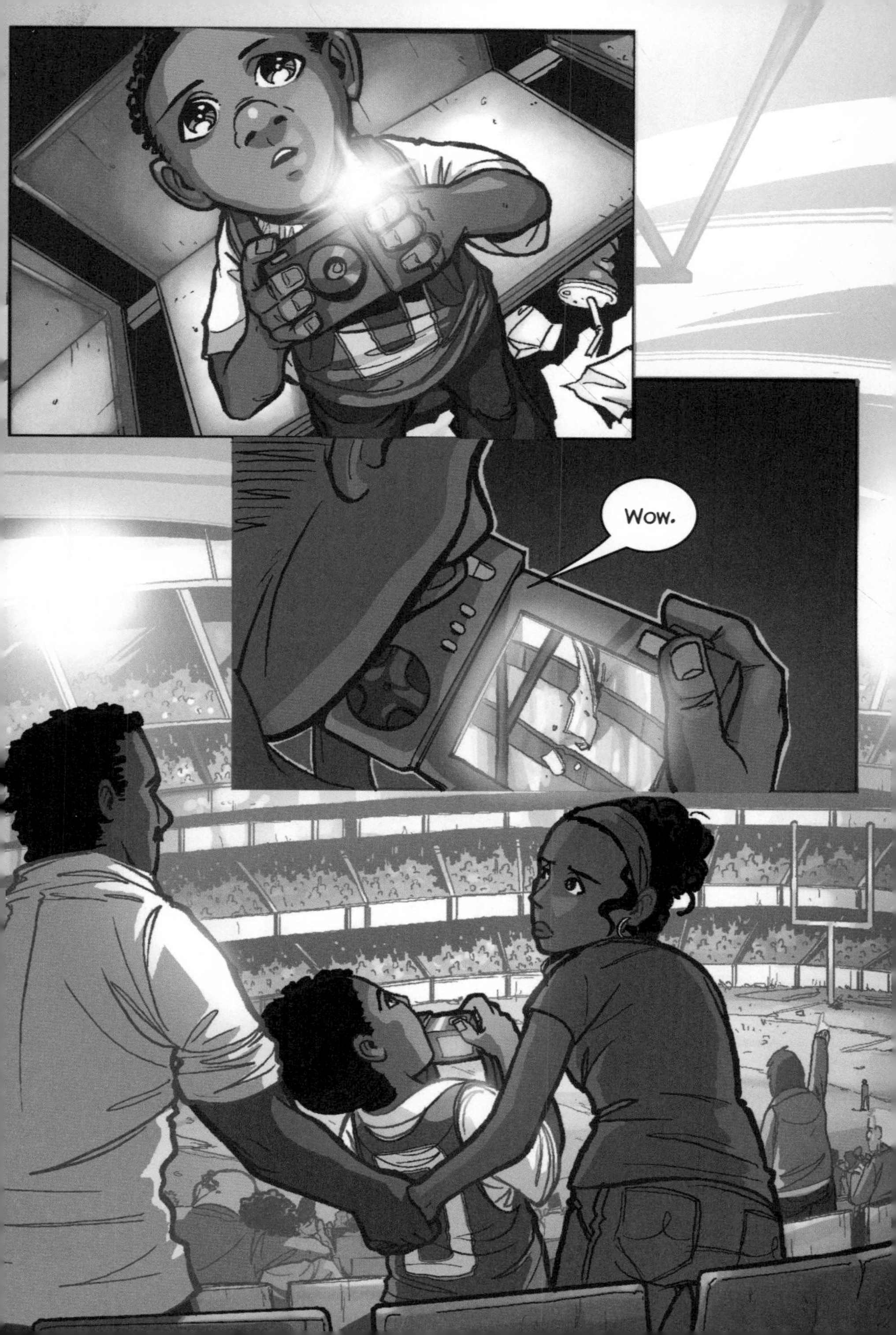
WOW.

Three days earlier, on August 26, 2006, Ricky's parents gave him the camera for his fourteenth birthday. He'd begged them for weeks but never really expected to get one. If he hadn't, Ricky wouldn't have minded. He had already received the greatest gift of all: A Saints game.

Ricky couldn't remember when his favorite football team, the New Orleans Saints, had ever played on his birthday. This year, his birthday fell on a Friday. The Saints were scheduled for a preseason showdown against the Indianapolis Colts. His Dad even made it home from work in time for kickoff.

By halftime, though, the Saints were down by 17 points. Even a new camera couldn't cheer Ricky up. "This is awful, Dad," said Ricky. "If the Saints lose today, it'll be the worst birthday ever."

"It could always be worse, Ricky," said his dad, pointing at the TV screen. "Look."

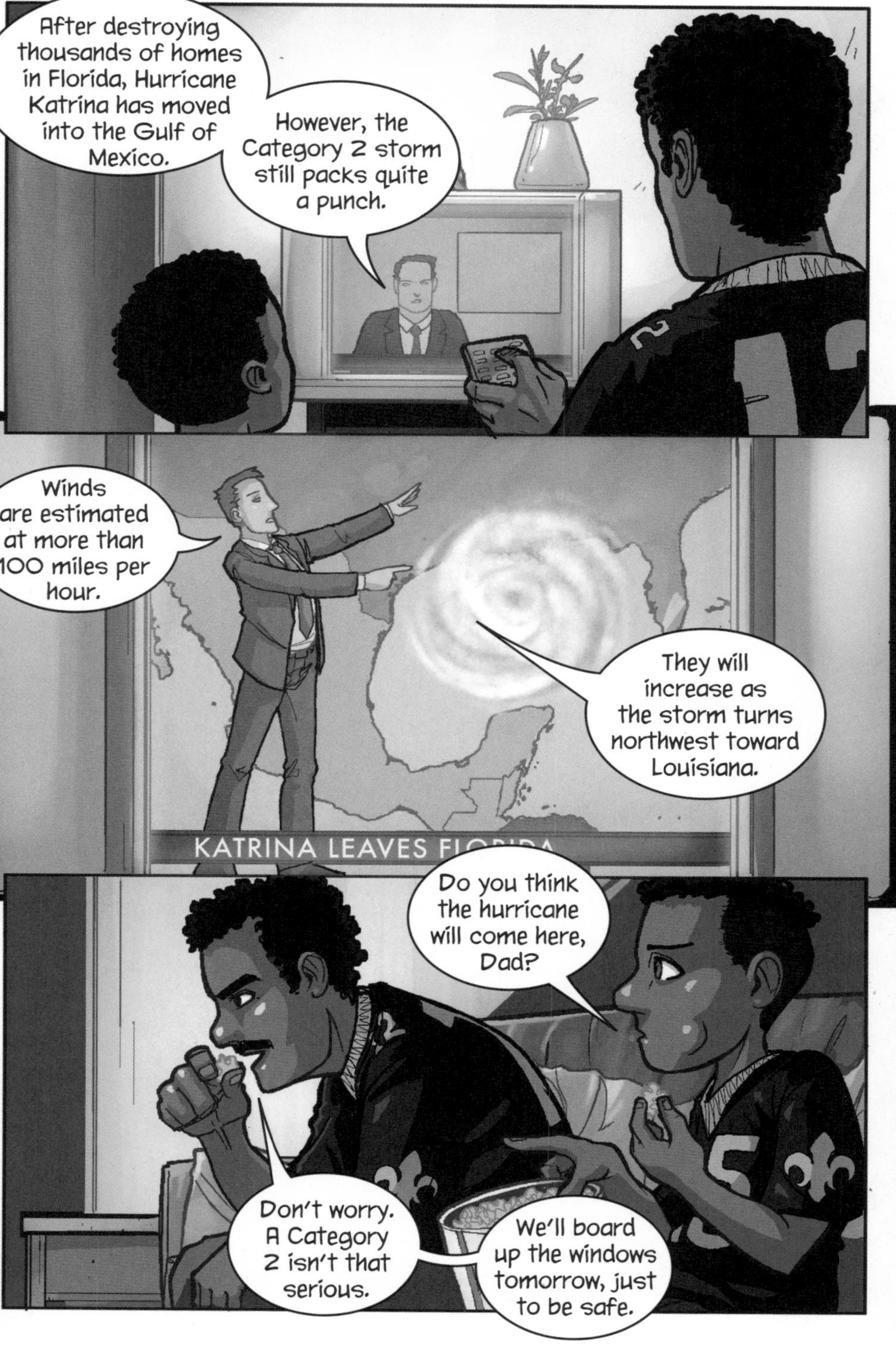
After destroying thousands of homes in Florida, Hurricane Katrina has moved into the Gulf of Mexico.
However, the Category 2 storm still packs quite a punch.
Winds are estimated at more than 100 miles per hour.
They will increase as the storm turns northwest toward Louisiana.
KATRINA LEAVES FLORIDA
Do you think the hurricane will come here, Dad?
Don't worry. A Category 2 isn't that serious.
We'll board up the windows tomorrow, just to be safe.

The next morning, Ricky awoke to the sound of pounding outside his window. At first, he thought his Dad was still stomping his feet after the Saints's 27–14 loss to the Colts. Then he remembered the weather reports.

Ricky jumped out of bed and rushed out of his bedroom. Halfway down the stairs, he stopped. "Come on, Bowzer!" Ricky yelled.

Seconds later, his five-year-old beagle scurried out of the bedroom doorway. The dog bolted past Ricky, leaping down the stairs, and stopping at the front door. Bowzer turned, wagging his tail with excitement.

"I'm coming, boy," Ricky said. He usually took the dog for a walk on Saturdays. Judging by last night's forecast, Ricky didn't think they would get a chance to walk today. But when he opened the door the sun was shining. In fact, the temperature was even hotter than the day before.

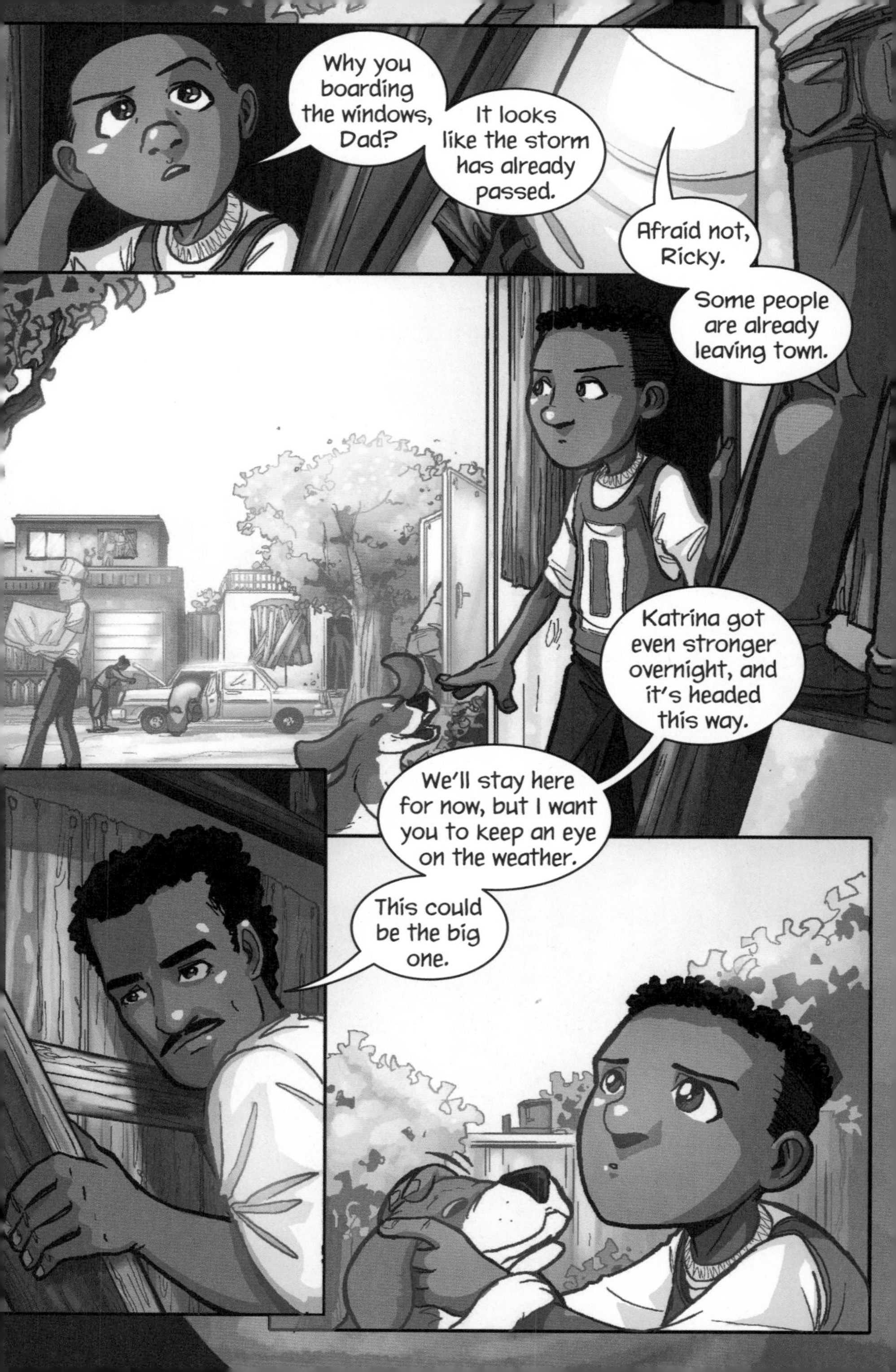
Why you boarding the windows, Dad?
It looks like the storm has already passed.
Afraid not, Ricky.
Some people are already leaving town.
Katrina got even stronger overnight, and it's headed this way.
We'll stay here for now, but I want you to keep an eye on the weather.
This could be the big one.

Ricky pulled Bowzer back inside the house. He sat down on the living room couch and flicked on the television. As his mother made breakfast in the kitchen, he watched for the latest updates.

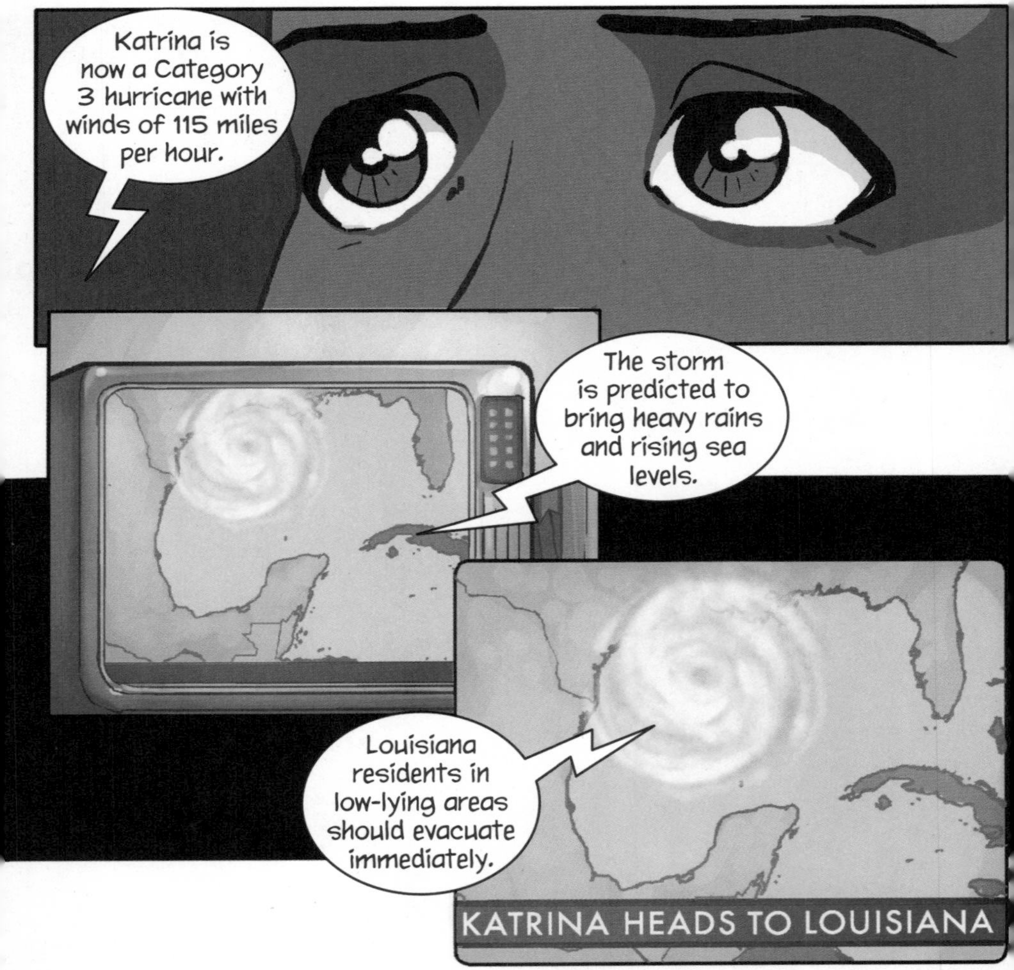
Katrina is now a Category 3 hurricane with winds of 115 miles per hour.
The storm is predicted to bring heavy rains and rising sea levels.
Louisiana residents in low-lying areas should evacuate immediately.
KATRINA HEADS TO LOUISIANA

As the hours passed, Ricky watched as the forecast for his city became worse. He knew that New Orleans was built several feet below sea level. A system of canals, levees, and flood walls kept water away from streets and neighborhoods.

Normally, this system worked just fine. But Hurricane Katrina wasn't a normal storm. Heavy rain, wind, and waves could cause the sea level to rise unusually high. For a city built below sea level, a massive storm meant disaster.

At nearly five o'clock in the afternoon, Ricky's stomach growled. He hadn't eaten all day. He hadn't fed Bowzer either.

"Come on, boy," said Ricky. "You must be starving." He gave Bowzer a pat on the head and started toward the kitchen. Suddenly, the weather reports were interrupted by a special bulletin.

"Mom! Dad!" Ricky said. "The mayor's on TV!"

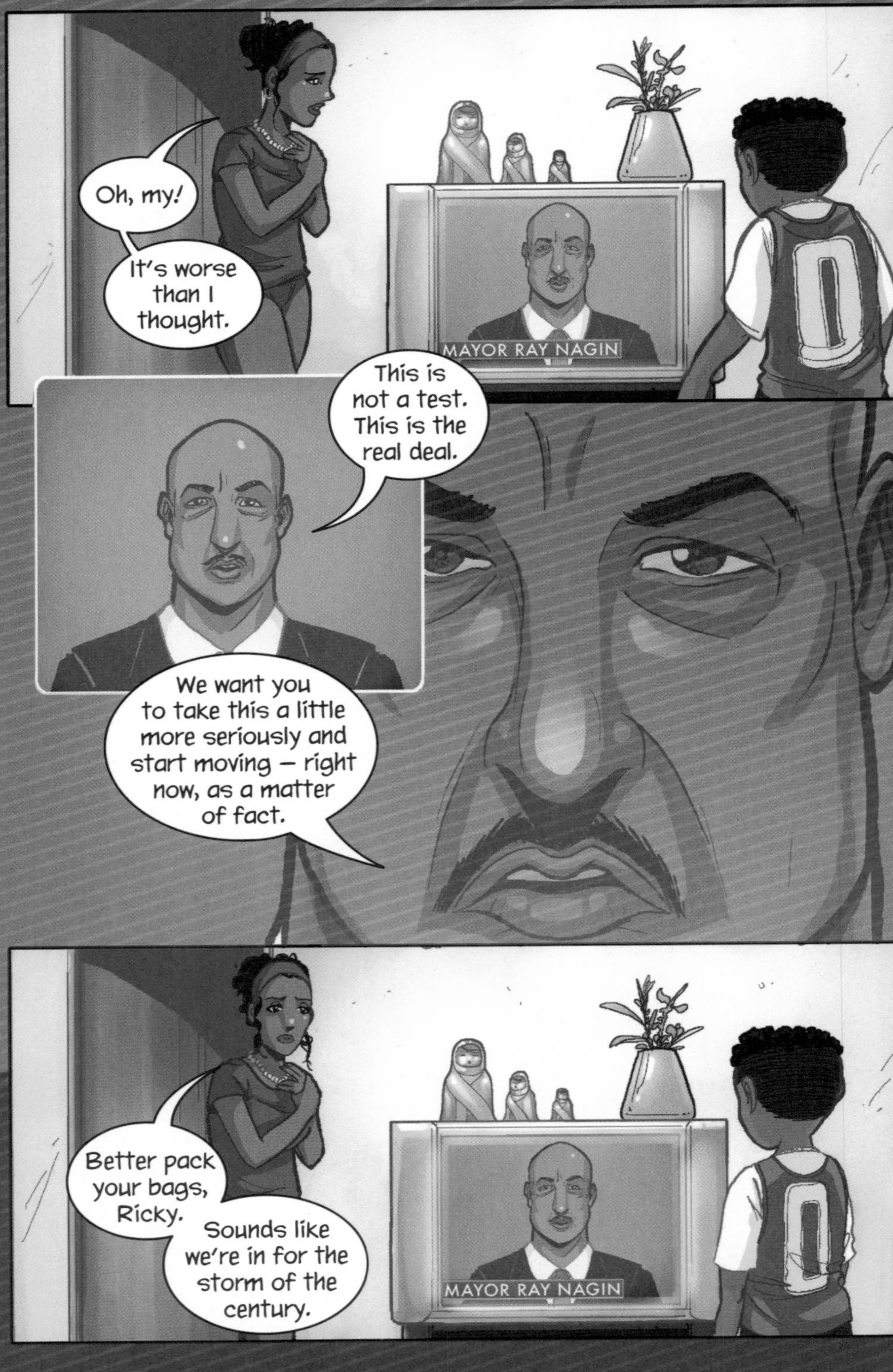
Oh, my!
It's worse than I thought.
MAYOR RAY NAGIN
This is not a test. This is the real deal.
We want you to take this a little more seriously and start moving — right now, as a matter of fact.
Better pack your bags, Ricky.
Sounds like we're in for the storm of the century.
MAYOR RAY NAGIN

CHAPTER 2

LEAVING TOWN

That night, Ricky sat in his room, looking out at the darkened sky. His parents told him to pack a few things and get some sleep. They would leave in the morning to find a hotel in the northern part of Louisiana.

Ricky scanned his room. He didn't have much, but he couldn't fit everything in his backpack either. His Saints football, his video games, and his favorite books would all get left behind.

When he was finished packing, Ricky knew he couldn't possibly sleep. Instead, he pulled out his new digital camera. He took picture after picture, capturing everything he couldn't bring along.

Late that night, the storm still hadn't hit, and Ricky finally dozed off to sleep. When he woke up the next morning, his toes were soaking wet. He sprang up in bed, looking down at his feet.

"What's the matter, boy," said Ricky. His dog Bowzer was frantically licking at his toes. "Do you need to go outside?"

Ricky got out of bed and walked toward his bedroom window. "Maybe we should check the weather first. Huh, boy?" he said.

Ricky thought for sure that the wind and rain would have started already. But when he looked outside, the weather still hadn't changed. The sun was starting to rise, and the trees outside weren't blowing around at all.

"Looks like you're in luck," he said. "Come on, boy." Ricky grabbed his backpack and headed downstairs. His loyal dog followed closely behind.

Ricky's mother met him at the bottom of the stairs. "I was just about to wake you," she said. "The storm is getting closer, and your father wants to get moving. Do you have everything?"

Ricky nodded, raising his backpack into the air. "Oh, I almost forgot Bowzer's leash," he said.

"Ricky," his mother began. She grabbed her son before he could walk away. "We can't take Bowzer with us."

"But why?" asked Ricky. "I promise he'll be good. Won't you, boy?" He kneeled down and rubbed his dog's head.

"I know, Ricky," she said. "But it'll be tough finding a hotel room, and even tougher with the dog along."

"But what if —," Ricky started to say and then stopped. He knew he couldn't argue with his mother.

"Don't worry," his mother said. "Our neighbor, Mr. Robertson, said he'd drop Bowzer at the local shelter. We'll pick him up when we get back."

Ricky removed the new camera strapped around his neck. He handed it to his mother.

"All right," Ricky said softly. He lifted Bowzer off of the ground. As he rubbed the dog's head, Ricky's mother took a picture of the two of them together. "See you soon, buddy," Ricky whispered in his dog's ear.

Moments later, Ricky and his parents headed for the highway leading out of the city. Out in the Gulf of Mexico, Katrina had exploded into a massive Category 5 hurricane. It was racing due north — straight for New Orleans. The Thompsons were on the road to safety, a road that would take them away from Katrina.

Or so they thought.

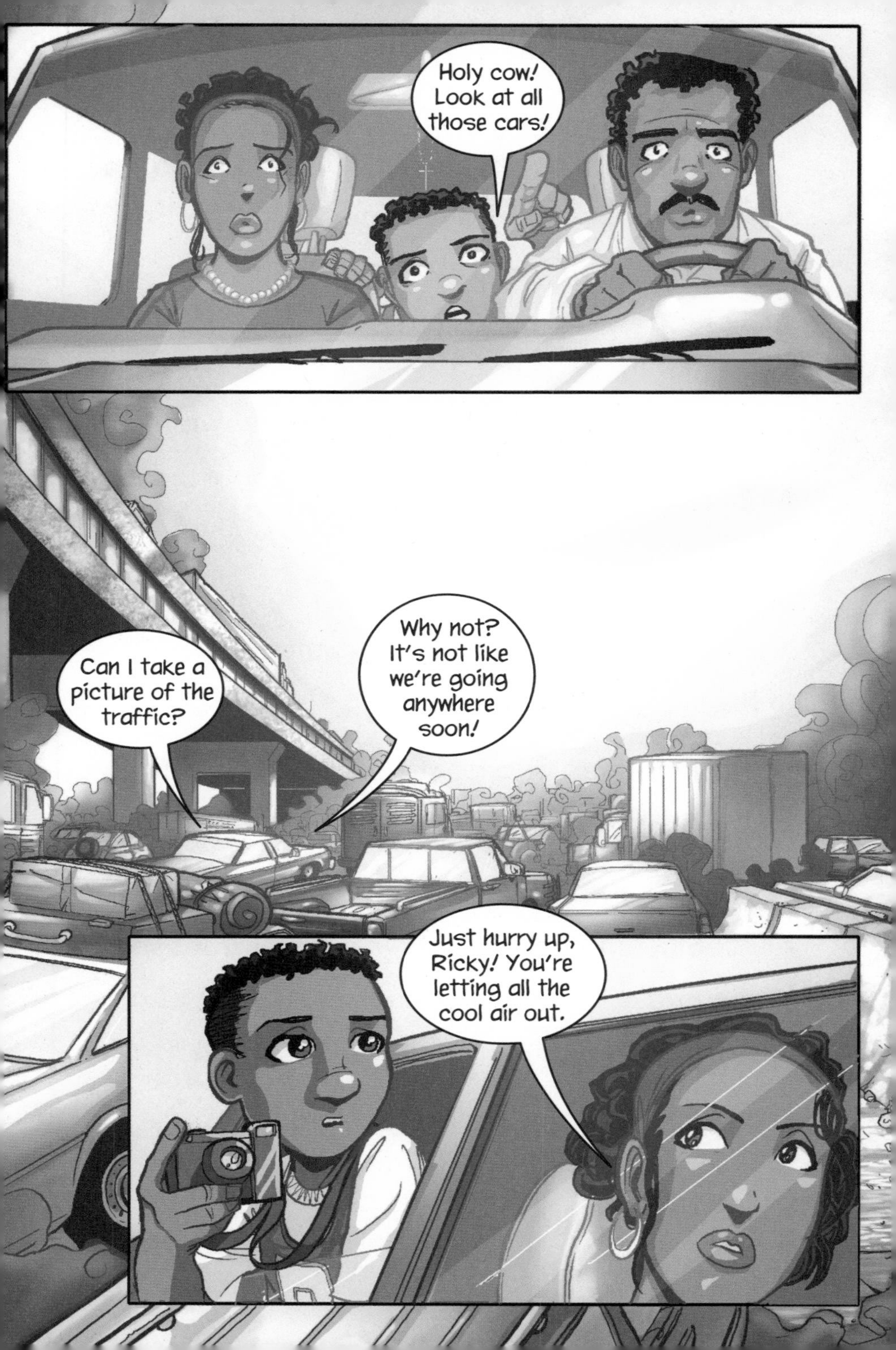
Holy cow! Look at all those cars!
Can I take a picture of the traffic?
Why not? It's not like we're going anywhere soon!
Just hurry up, Ricky! You're letting all the cool air out.

Unlike Ricky and his father, who had never lived anywhere but New Orleans, Ricky's mother had grown up in New England. Even though she'd been living in the South for more than ten years, she still wasn't used to the high temperatures. Whenever the thermostat was greater than seventy degrees, she was sure to be indoors where it was air conditioned.

Ricky sat back down and put up his window. "Want to see?" he asked, holding the camera out to his mother.

"Maybe later, honey," she said. She unfolded a map. "Right now, I'm — "

Bam! A loud bang from the front of the car stopped her in mid-sentence. There was a hissing sound and a puff of black smoke poured out from under the hood.

"Oh no," Mr. Thompson groaned.

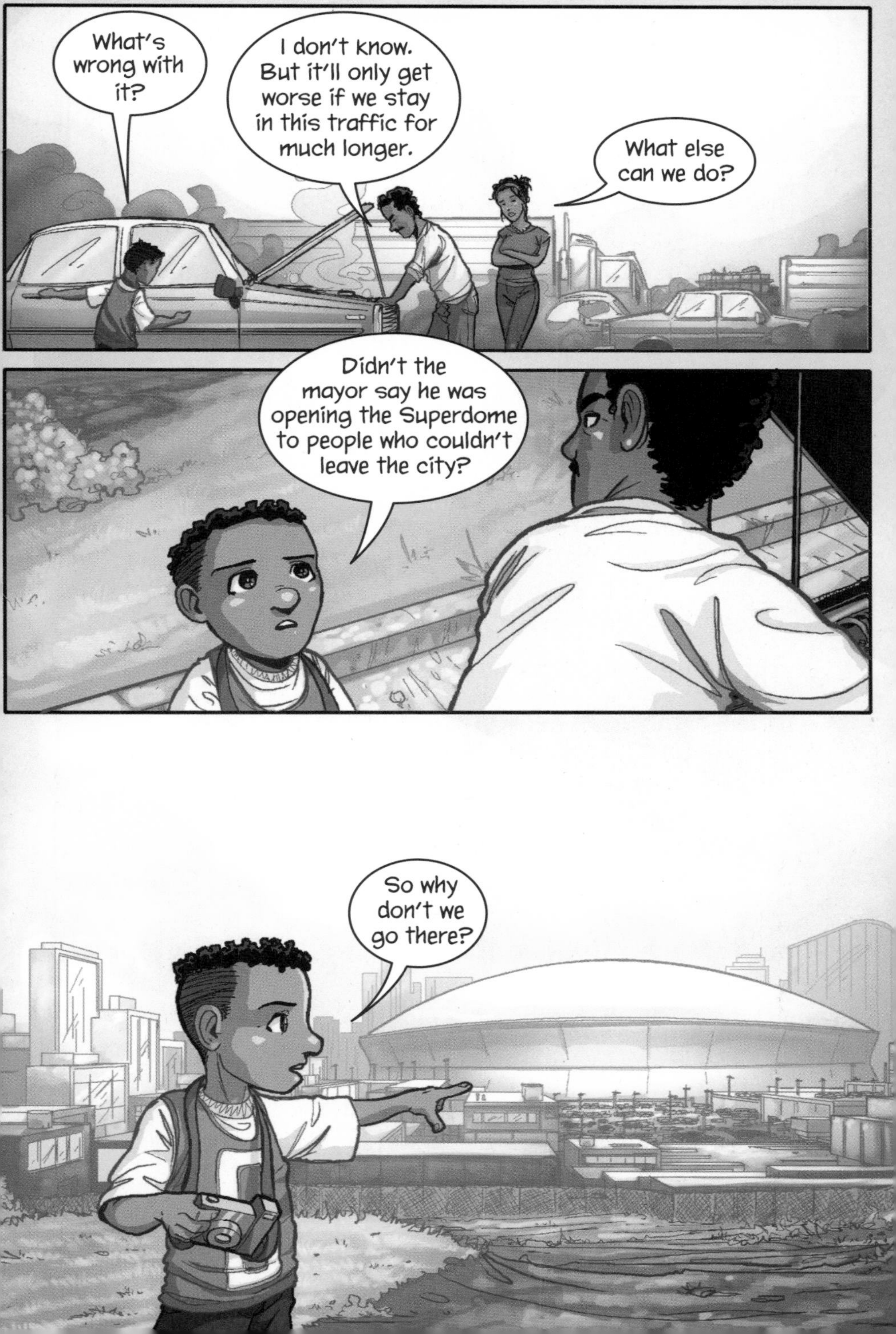
What's wrong with it?
I don't know. But it'll only get worse if we stay in this traffic for much longer.
What else can we do?
Didn't the mayor say he was opening the Superdome to people who couldn't leave the city?
So why don't we go there?

Mr. and Mrs. Thompson exchanged glances. "I guess we don't have a choice," his father said.

"It will only be until the storm is past," his mother agreed.

"Yeah," Ricky said. "And since we'll only be a few miles from our neighborhood, we'll be back home before anyone else! We can get Bowzer sooner, too," he added.

Mr. Thompson started up the car again. "Cross your fingers that the car doesn't die before we get to the Dome," he said grimly. "Otherwise, we'll have to walk."

The car coughed and wheezed to the next exit. Fortunately, they made it to a nearby parking area. They unloaded their luggage and set off for the stadium.

CHAPTER 3

THE SUPERDOME

"Wow!" Ricky cried as they turned a corner. "The lines of people here are as long as the lines of cars on the highway!"

It was true. Rows of hot, tired people started at the Superdome's main gates and snaked far down the street. Ricky snapped a photo and then joined his parents in line.

"Excuse me," his mother asked the person in front of her. "Do you know what's taking so long?'

"The National Guard is searching everyone before they let them inside," the man said.

"What are they looking for?" Ricky asked.

"Weapons, I suppose," the man said.

The man pointed at Ricky's camera. "I suggest you keep that with you at all times, son."

"Why?" Ricky asked.

"Someone might steal it, that's why!" he said.

Ricky swallowed hard. He edged a little closer to his father.

Time crawled by the rest of the afternoon. By one o'clock, sweat prickled Ricky's scalp and trickled down his back. By two o'clock, an elderly woman behind them collapsed from heat and exhaustion. A National Guardsman appeared and carried her away. Where, Ricky didn't know.

Finally, just before four o'clock, they reached the stadium's entrance. A uniformed soldier checked their luggage and patted them down.

Just before entering the front gates, Ricky felt a raindrop hit his forehead. He looked up at the sky, which had darkened with swirling clouds.

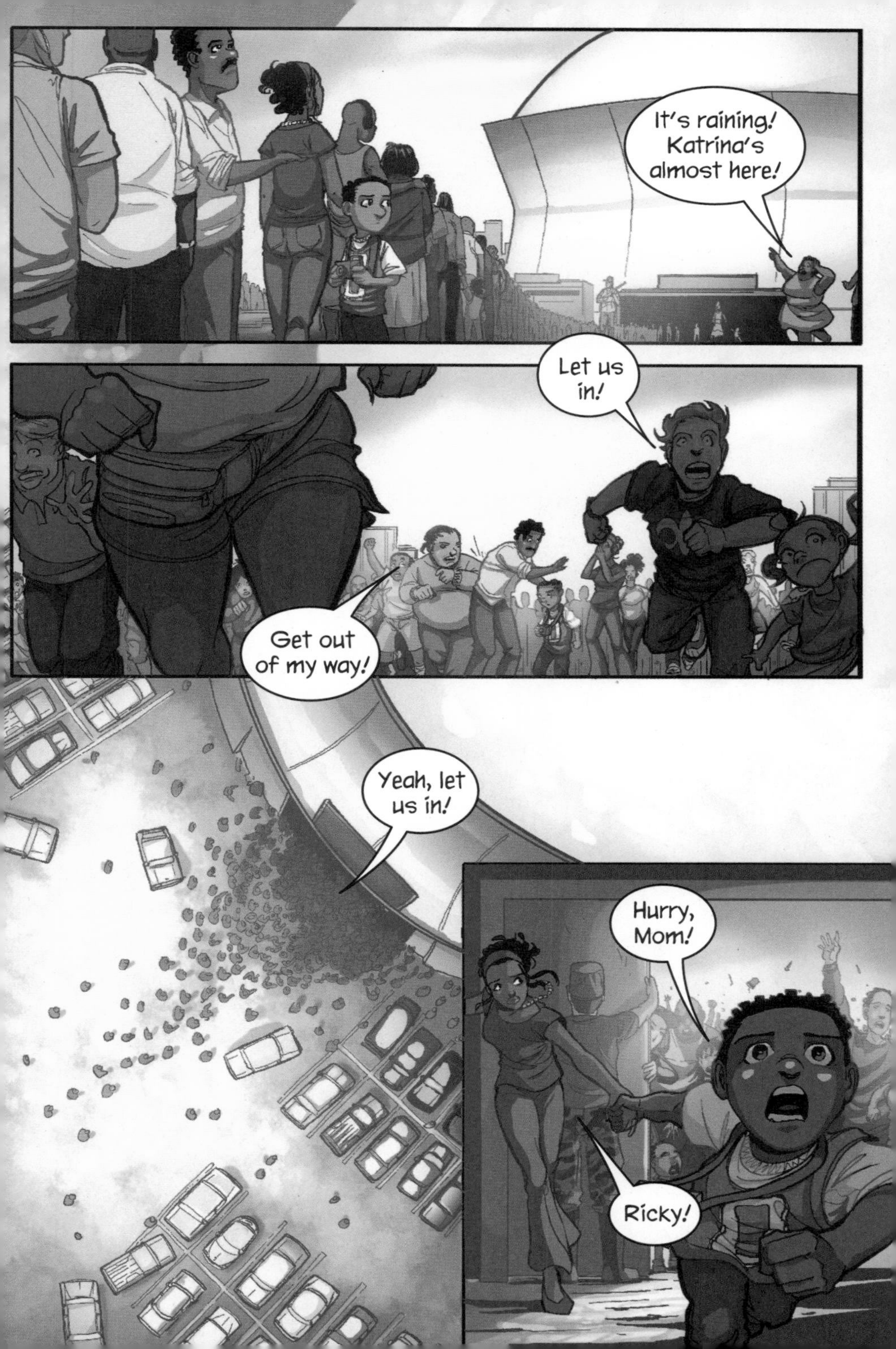
It's raining! Katrina's almost here!
Let us in!
Get out of my way!
Yeah, let us in!
Hurry, Mom!
Ricky!

As heavy rain started to fall, Ricky and his parents slipped inside the Superdome. He had been there many times to watch the Saints play. He loved the stadium's curved concrete ceiling and its green-and-white turf. He loved its bright lights and its smells of fried food.

"Hey, Dad, after the storm could we get tickets for . . ." Ricky's voice died as he walked into the main stadium. His jaw dropped.

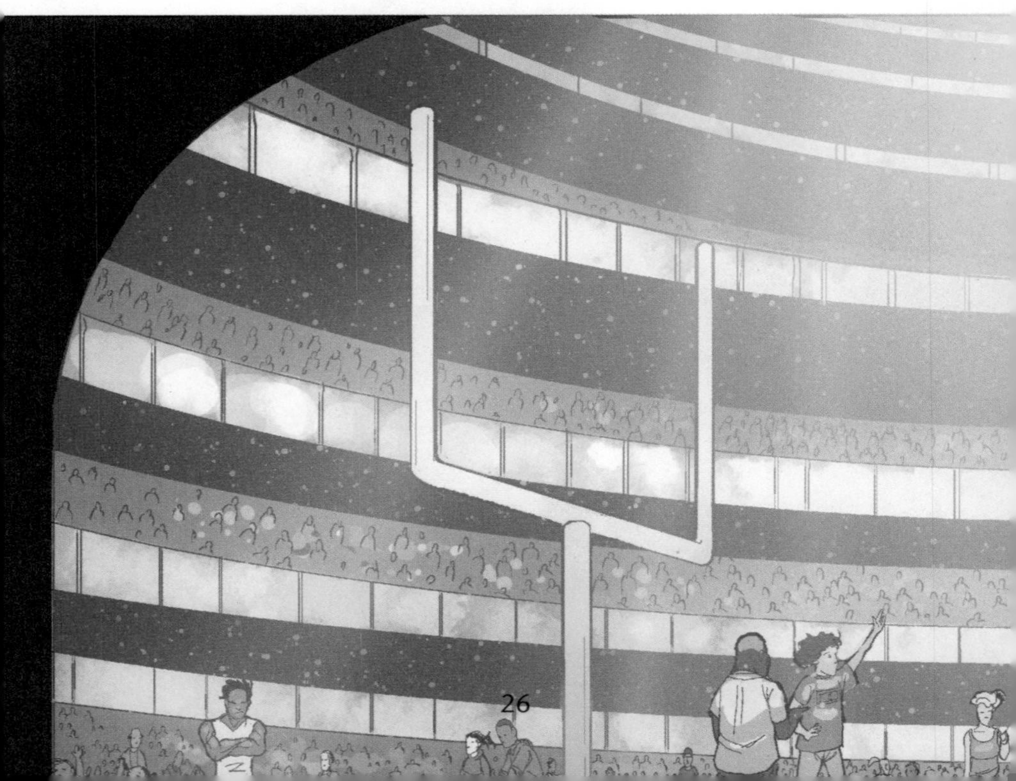

There were people everywhere. They were setting up makeshift campsites and carrying suitcases, clothes, blankets, toys, backpacks, and even garbage bags stuffed with their belongings. Babies cried, children shrieked, men and women laughed, argued, and shouted. Food wrappers and containers, empty bottles and cans filled the trash. The smell of sweat mixed with a whiff of half-eaten food.

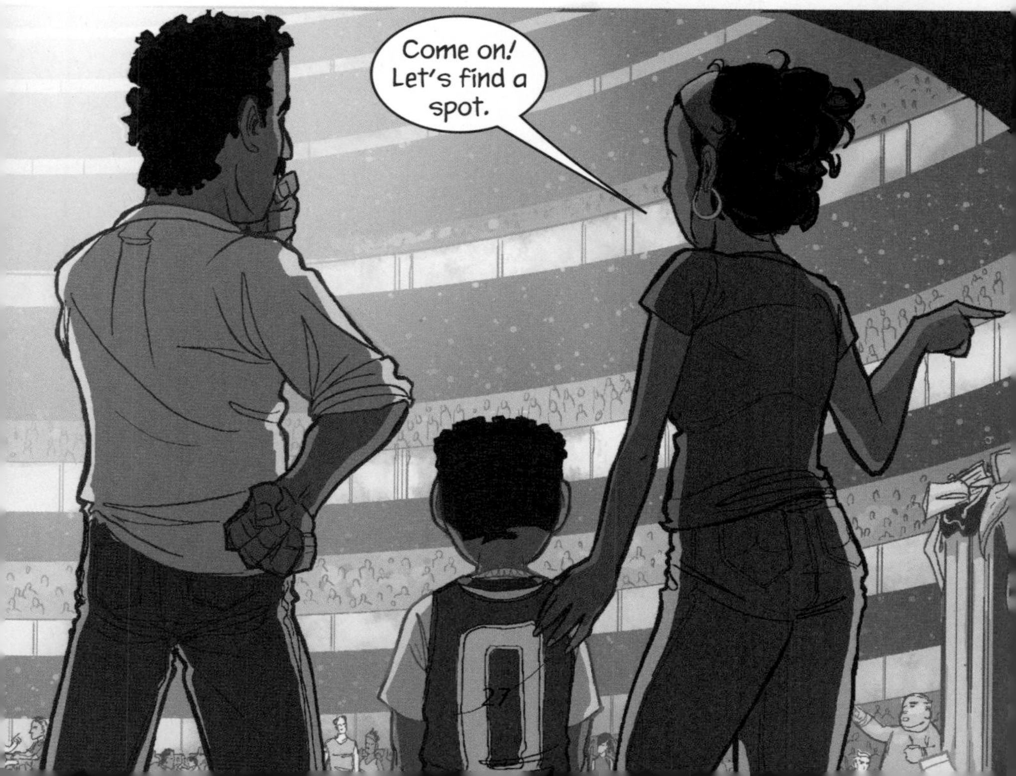
Come on! Let's find a spot.

The outer bands of the storm began to lash New Orleans long before Hurricane Katrina made landfall. As night fell, rain pelted the sidewalks and buildings. Wind tore through streets with increasing fury. It blasted shingles off of roofs, shattered windows, yanked branches from trees, and hurled debris everywhere. Nothing was safe.

Inside the Superdome, Ricky couldn't really hear the storm. There were simply too many people around him, all trying to get comfortable in their strange surroundings.

Midway through the evening, the stadium's loudspeaker crackled. "Your attention, please. The lights of the Superdome will be dimmed at eleven o'clock tonight," a voice said. "Food will be available tomorrow morning at seven o'clock."

Ricky and his parents settled down for the night. Ricky was sure he'd never fall asleep. But when the lights faded as scheduled, he dozed off.

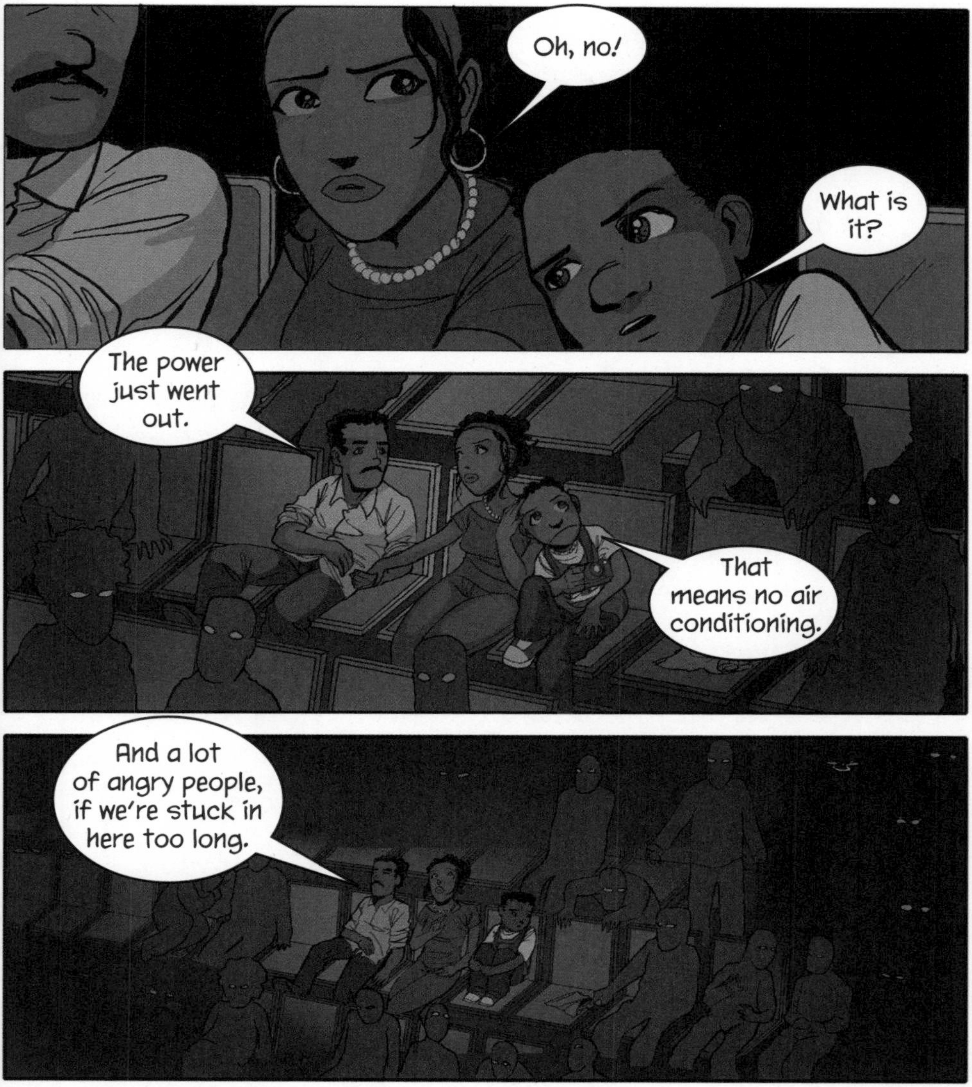
Oh, no!
What is it?
The power just went out.
That means no air conditioning.
And a lot of angry people, if we're stuck in here too long.

Ricky thought about weapons and swallowed hard. Suddenly, yesterday's long wait outside the Superdome while the Guards searched everyone made complete sense.

Ricky's father left them to stand in line for their ready-to-eat breakfast meals. When he returned an hour later, he told them that Katrina had made landfall at six o'clock that morning. "The worst of the storm is raging through New Orleans right now," he said.

Ricky looked at his watch. It was nearly nine o'clock. At that very moment — *boom! boom! boom!* — Hurricane Katrina unleashed its monstrous power on the roof of the Superdome!

"It sounds like a freight train!" someone yelled.

"What if the whole roof comes off?" another cried. "What will we do?"

Luckily, no more holes appeared. But nothing could stop the water that flooded into the Dome. It turned the turf below into a soggy sea of green. The people who had been staying in that section were forced to move.

Ricky watched those people trudge to drier ground. He knew how they felt. He was hot, tired, and bored. He was hungry for a home-cooked meal. He wanted to sleep in his own bed. And he missed Bowzer. Ricky picked up his camera and scanned through the images until he found the one of his dog.

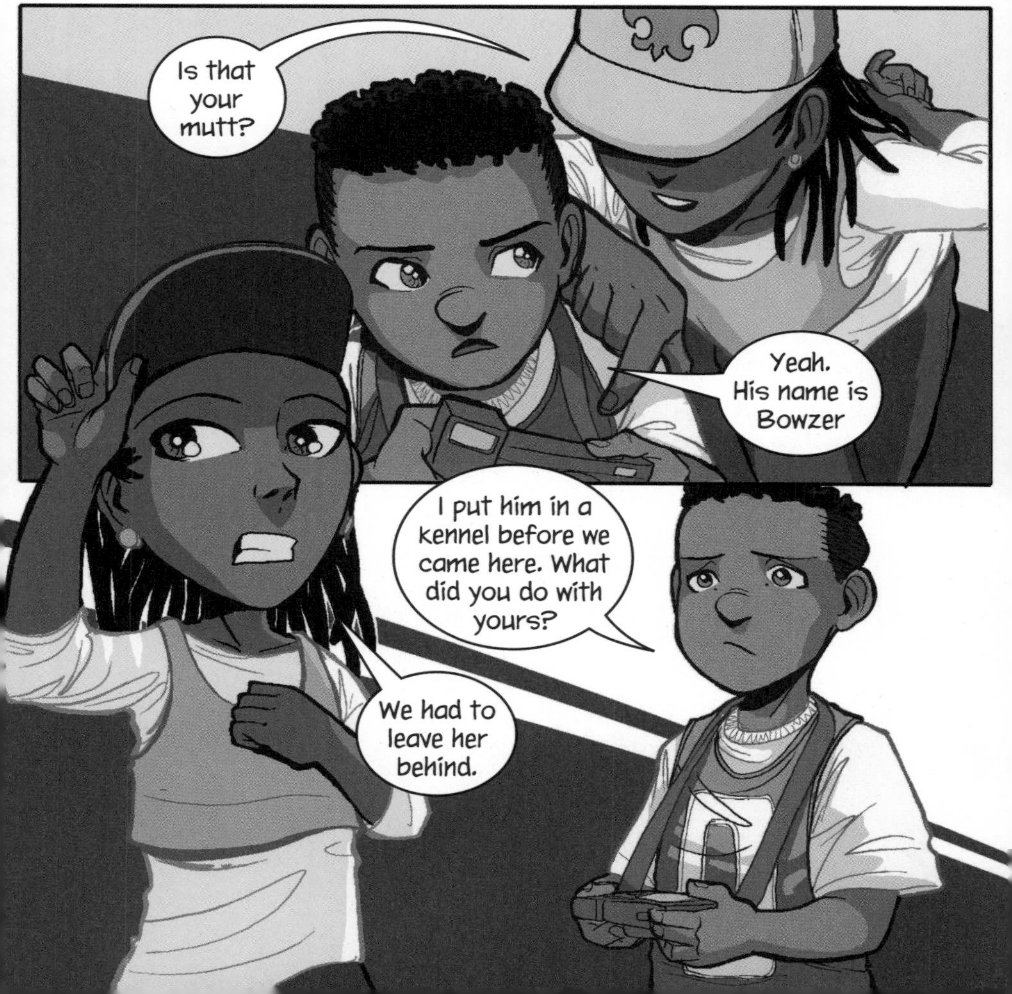
Is that your mutt?
Yeah. His name is Bowzer
I put him in a kennel before we came here. What did you do with yours?
We had to leave her behind.

Ricky didn't know what to say. He couldn't imagine leaving Bowzer at home by himself for more than a few hours. He knew the girl must be worried sick.

"What's your dog's name?" he finally asked.

"Saint," the girl replied.

"Like the football team!" Ricky exclaimed.

"Yep, and I'm Cleo," the girl said.

"I'm Ricky," he replied. "I live in Lakeview. Where do you live?"

Cleo named a street in a section of the city known as the Lower Ninth Ward. "You know it?"

Ricky shook his head. "New Orleans is a big place," he said. "There are lots of streets I've never heard of." He picked up his camera. "Want me to take your picture?"

Cleo shrugged. "I guess," she said.

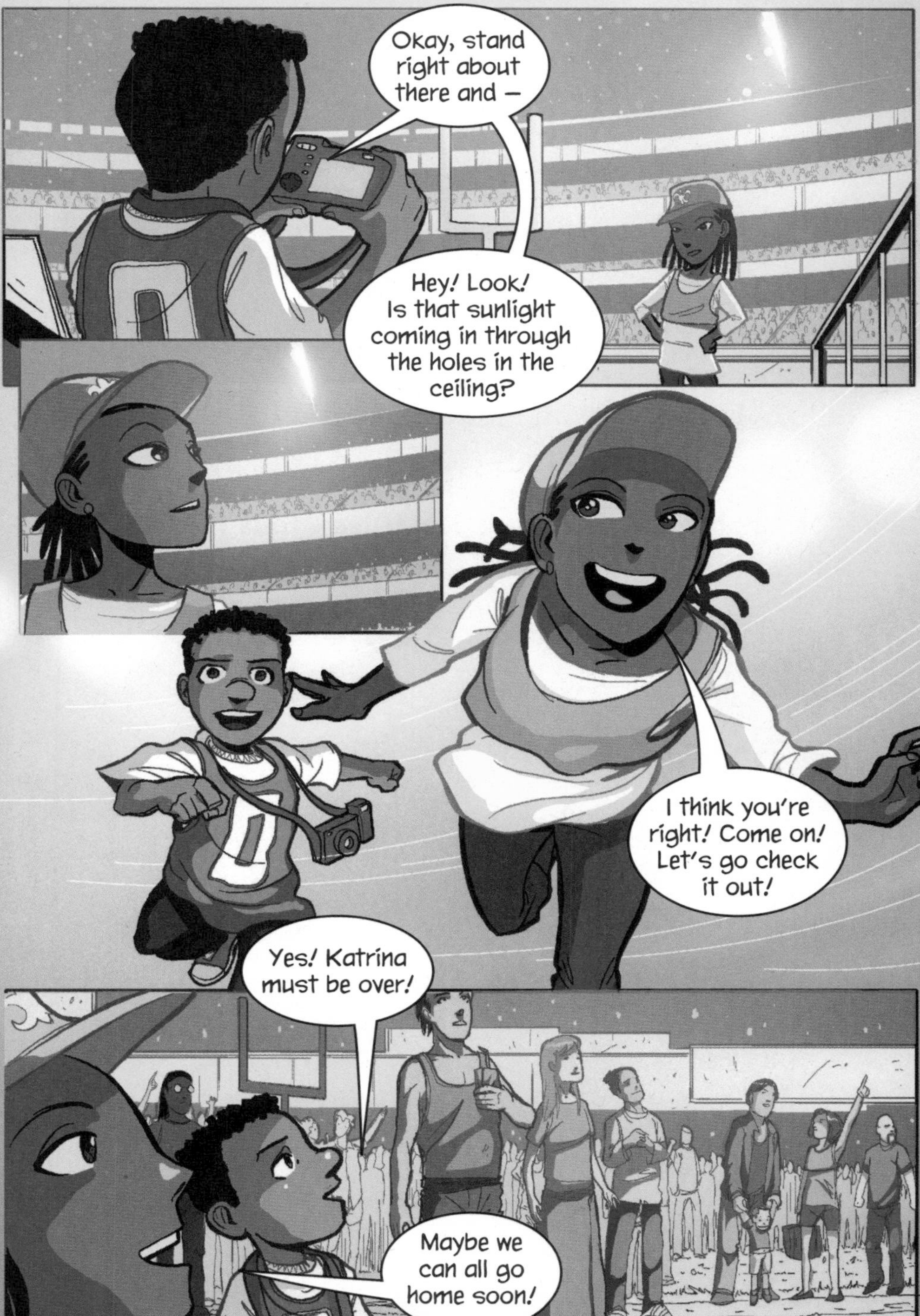
Okay, stand right about there and –
Hey! Look! Is that sunlight coming in through the holes in the ceiling?
I think you're right! Come on! Let's go check it out!
Yes! Katrina must be over!
Maybe we can all go home soon!

CHAPTER 4

NO WAY OUT

What Ricky didn't know was that the homes they longed to return to no longer existed. Hours before, Hurricane Katrina's winds ripped the Superdome roof apart. Its storm surge punched massive gaps in the levees and flood walls protecting New Orleans from the water surrounding it.

Millions of gallons of water gushed through those gaps throughout the morning. Floodwaters swept into streets and neighborhoods all day and all night, destroying everything in their path.

By early Tuesday morning, nearly all of New Orleans was submerged.

When Ricky woke up, he had no idea what had happened in his city. He grinned happily. The storm was over. He'd get Bowzer back today, and tonight he'd sleep in his very own bed!

Then he glanced at his mother and his smile faded. Her hair was a tangled mess. Her clothes were rumpled. She didn't look well.

Then she opened her eyes and smiled at him. "Hi kiddo," she whispered.

"Hi, Mom," he whispered back. He picked up his camera. "I have to use the bathroom."

Mrs. Thompson sat up. "So do I," she said.

They weaved their way through the maze of cots to the restrooms. Ricky's mother disappeared into the women's room. Ricky pushed open the men's room door.

The stink was like nothing he'd ever smelled before. He gagged and let the door close.

"That bad, huh?" a deep voice said. It was a National Guardsman.

"Yes, sir," Ricky replied. "I think something's wrong with one of the toilets."

"Something's wrong with all of them," the Guard said. "Come on. I'll go in with you. Get a lungful of air and — go!"

Ricky held his breath while he used the toilet. He rushed back out as quickly as he could.

His mother was waiting. She looked ill. When she saw the Guard she said, "Don't tell me. The water pressure in the building is failing, right? That's why the toilets won't flush."

The man nodded. "That's not the worst of it."

He led them to a glassed-in area of the Superdome. Normally, the area looked out onto pavement and roads. Now it looked out onto a sea of filthy, green water.

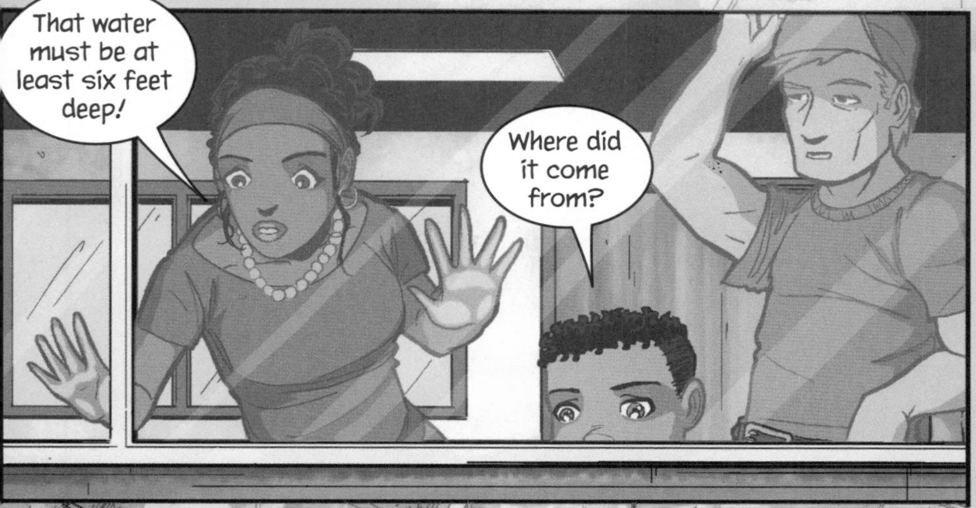
That water must be at least six feet deep!
Where did it come from?

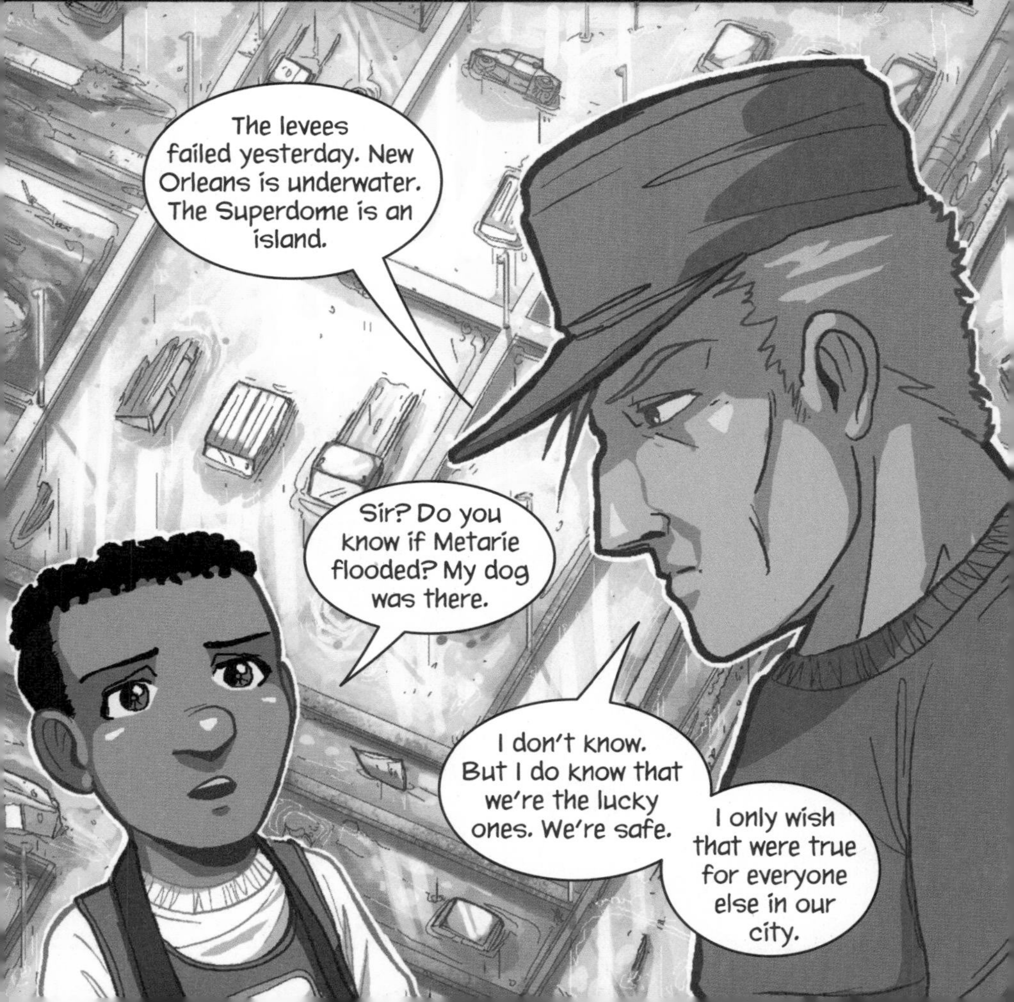
The levees failed yesterday. New Orleans is underwater. The Superdome is an island.
Sir? Do you know if Metarie flooded? My dog was there.
I don't know. But I do know that we're the lucky ones. We're safe.
I only wish that were true for everyone else in our city.

As Tuesday morning stretched into Tuesday afternoon, the Superdome became a sauna. The heat, plus the smell, made the people inside desperate.

Some relief came when the National Guard opened the Dome's outer walkway. Ricky and hundreds of other evacuees stepped outside for their first breath of fresh air in days.

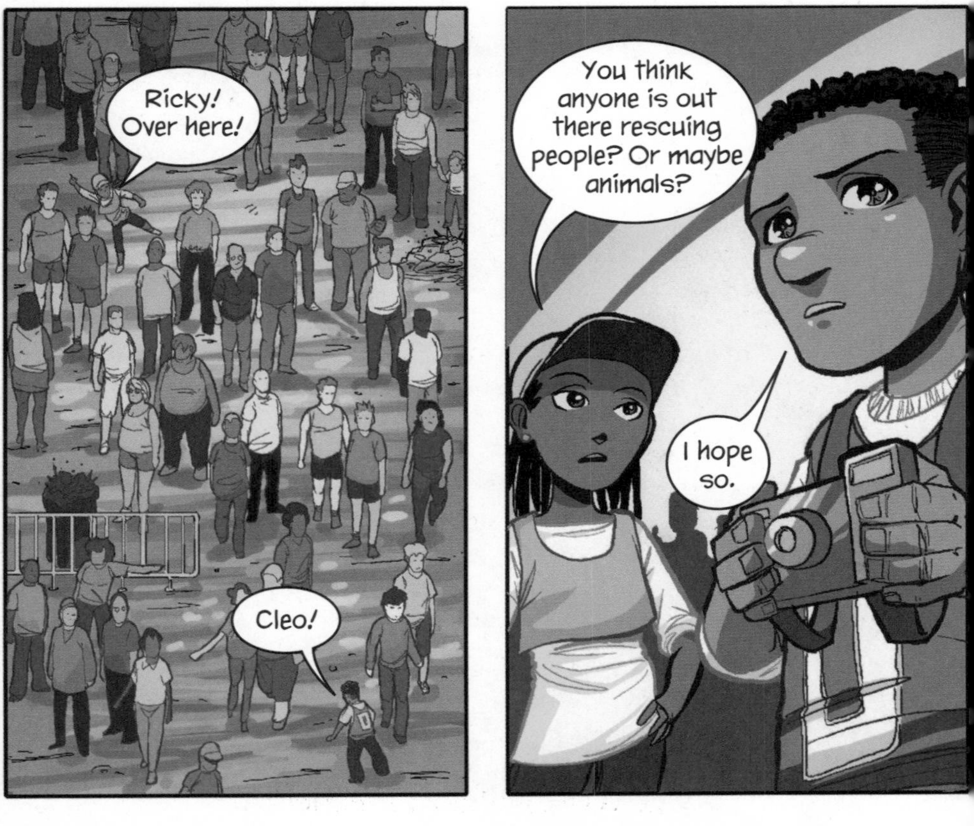
Ricky! Over here!
Cleo!
You think anyone is out there rescuing people? Or maybe animals?
I hope so.

Just then, Ricky heard a loud noise from below. Looking down, he saw a boat filled with men, women, and children chugging toward the stadium. Four National Guardsmen waded through the water to help the people out. Ricky zoomed in and snapped their picture.

As the boat slowly spun away from the Superdome, Cleo glanced at the tiny camera screen and gasped. "I know that little girl!" she said. "She and her grandfather live in my neighborhood! Maybe they saw Saint! Come on!"

She dashed inside with Ricky on her heels.

"Cleo! Is that you, child?" an old man cried.

Cleo hurried to the man's side. "It's me, Mr. Benoit. Are you and Lisa okay?"

Mr. Benoit rubbed his face with his hands. "When the floodwaters came, we went to the attic," he said. "But the water just kept rising."

"What did you do?" Ricky asked.

"I chopped through the attic ceiling with my axe," he said. "We climbed out onto the roof. If we hadn't, we would have drowned for sure."

"You're lucky you had a roof to climb onto," said a woman beside them. "Katrina tore mine clear off and smashed it to pieces."

Cleo turned to the little girl. "How are you, Lisa?" she asked softly.

Lisa burst into tears. "My grandpa made me swim in that water!" she said. "It smelled really, really bad. I saw my kitty swimming in it, too. She doesn't even like clean water." Lisa gazed up at Cleo. "Do you think I'll ever see her again?"

"I sure hope so, Lisa." Cleo's voice cracked.

Ricky leaned toward the old man. "Mr. Benoit, did you see Cleo's dog, Saint?" he asked.

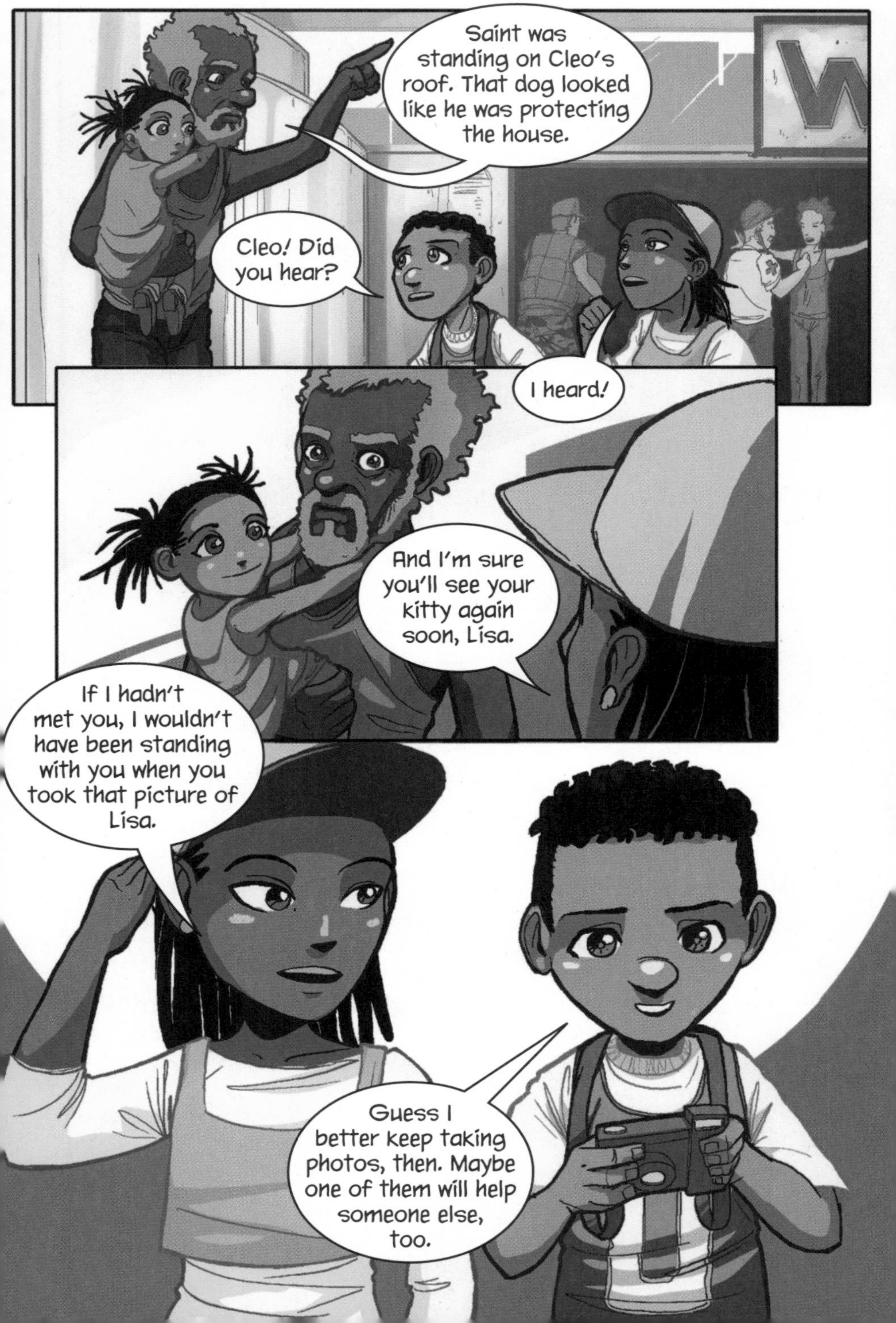
Saint was standing on Cleo's roof. That dog looked like he was protecting the house.
Cleo! Did you hear?
I heard!
And I'm sure you'll see your kitty again soon, Lisa.
If I hadn't met you, I wouldn't have been standing with you when you took that picture of Lisa.
Guess I better keep taking photos, then. Maybe one of them will help someone else, too.

CHAPTER 5

AFTERMATH

Ricky did keep taking photos. He took pictures of the refugees as they arrived by the thousands. Some had walked, slogging through knee-deep water to the Dome's entrance. Others came by truck, by boat, and even by helicopter. By Wednesday, the Superdome was filled to the bursting point with exhausted, desperate people.

Ricky snapped shots of people sleeping in the halls of the Superdome. He photographed the trash that littered every part of the Dome. He took pictures outside, too.

The camera, however, couldn't record the smell of rotting garbage and of human waste. The stench hung like a thick cloud over everything.

The camera couldn't record the heat that climbed ever higher Wednesday. And it couldn't record the growing frustration of those in charge.

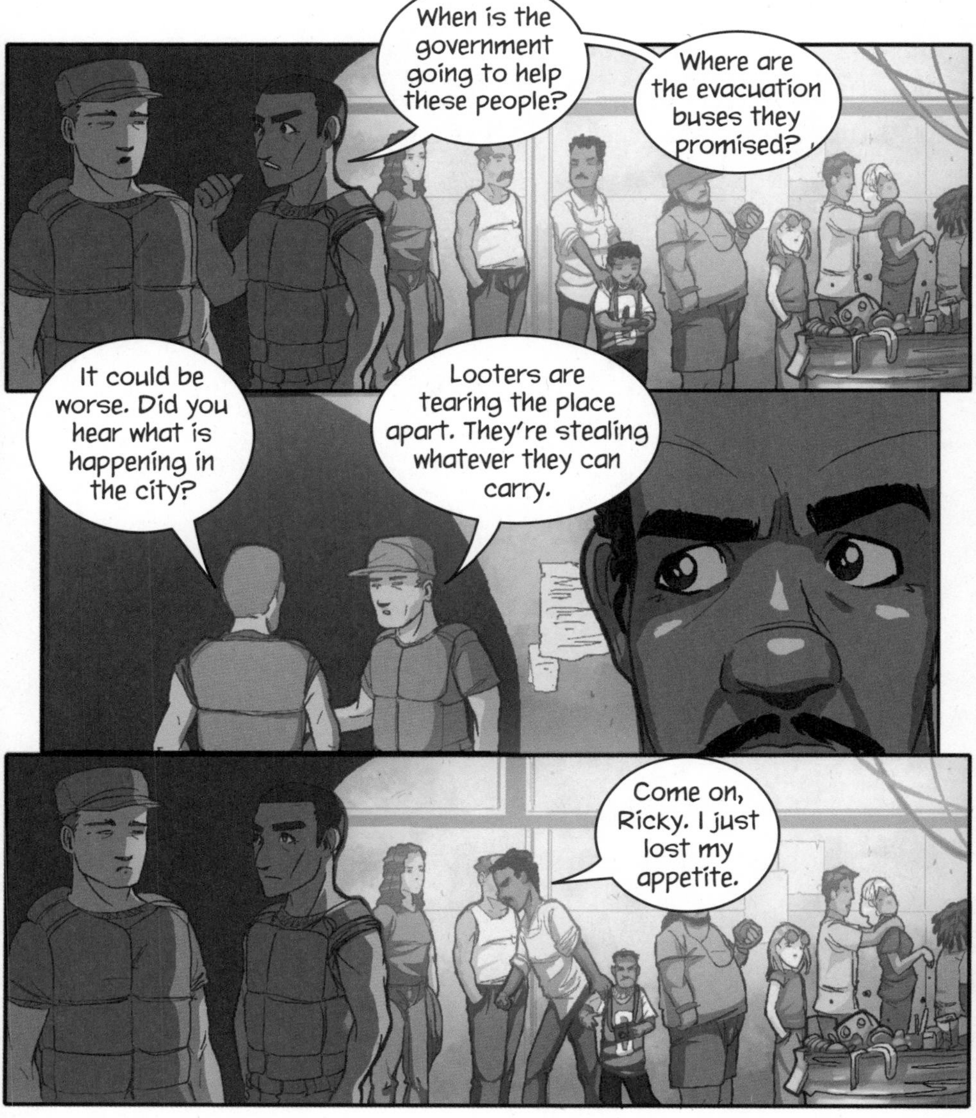
When is the government going to help these people?
Where are the evacuation buses they promised?
It could be worse. Did you hear what is happening in the city?
Looters are tearing the place apart. They're stealing whatever they can carry.
Come on, Ricky. I just lost my appetite.

After breakfast, Ricky's family stood on the walkway. Ricky wondered if he'd see Cleo again. Then he realized it would be like finding a needle in a haystack. There were just too many people.

Outside, floodwaters surrounding the Dome had started to go down. But in their wake, they had left a deep sea of trash.

"Dad?" Ricky whispered as he stared at that debris. "When are we going to get out of here? And where are we going to go?"

"I'm not sure, Ricky," his father answered. "We just have to take it one step at a time."

Their first step came on Thursday. Shortly after dawn, the refugees learned that plans were in place to evacuate them.

"Buses will be arriving at six this morning," the loudspeaker announced. "Evacuation will begin at this time."

Everyone immediately began gathering their belongings. Ricky tucked his camera into his pocket. He stuffed his filthy clothes into his suitcase, and he and his parents joined the groups of people moving toward the evacuation site. Then they waited beneath the baking sun.

Six o'clock came and went. No buses. Soon it was seven and then eight. Finally, at ten o'clock, the first buses arrived.

"At last," Mrs. Thompson said. She sat slumped on her suitcase.

"Where will they take us?" Ricky asked.

His father picked up his bag. "As long as it's away from here, I don't really care. Do you?"

"I do care, Dad," he replied. Ricky looked beyond the crowd of tired people. "I know Katrina probably wrecked everything we own, but until I know Bowzer is okay, I don't want to go too far."

Mr. Thompson pulled out his cell phone. "I have just enough juice left in the battery for one call. Maybe, just maybe, we'll be able to reach the kennel."

He dialed. Ricky held his breath. He prayed the call would go through.

It did! But it wasn't answered by a human being. Rather, a recorded voice spoke to Mr. Thompson.

"What's it saying?" Ricky asked.

Mr. Thompson handed him the phone. "Listen," he said.

". . . We have evacuated all animals in our care out of the city to our facility in Baton Rouge. Please contact us at your earliest convenience so you can be reunited with your pet."

As the voice read off a number, Ricky looked up at his father. "He got out," he said.

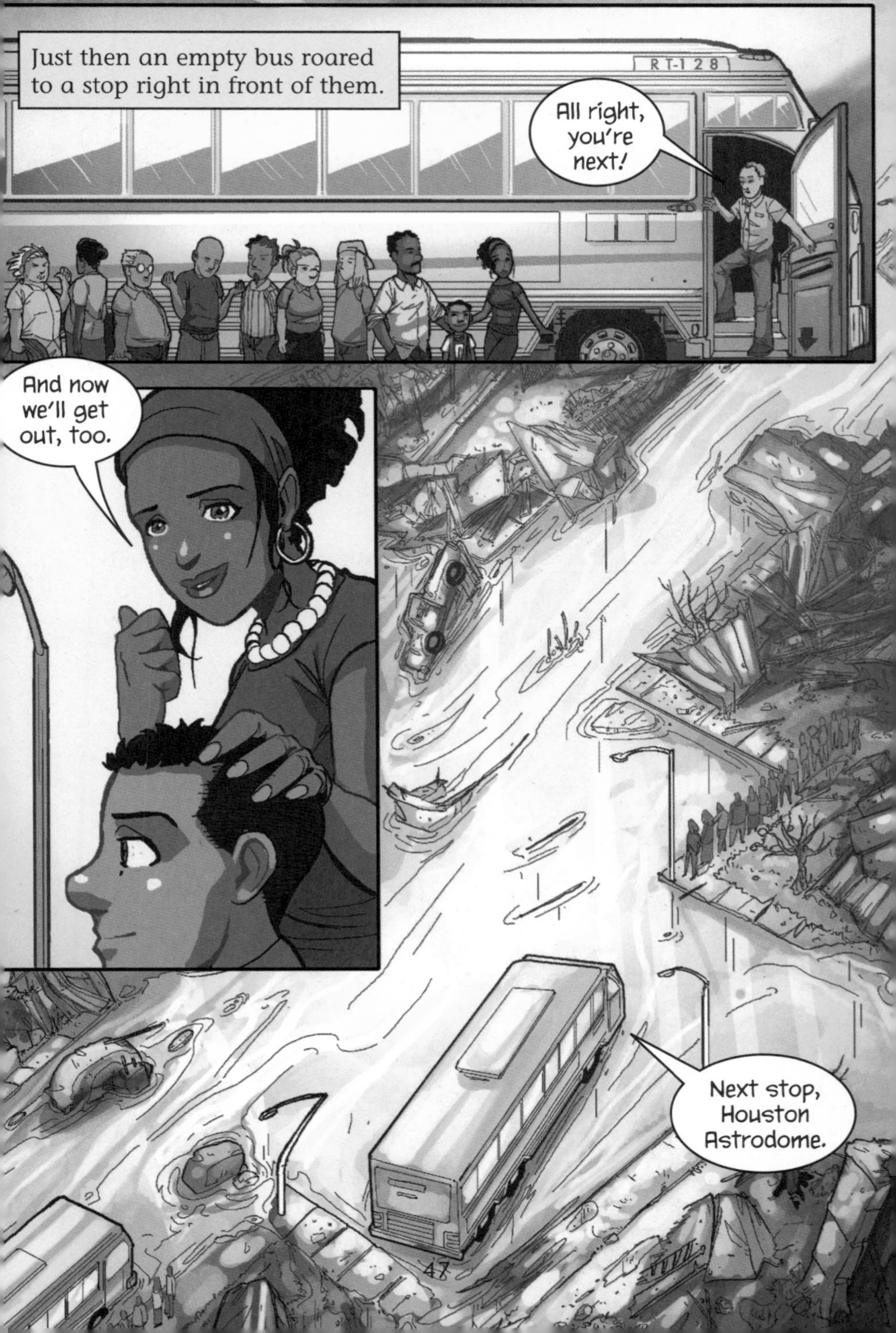
Just then an empty bus roared to a stop right in front of them.
RT-128
All right, you're next!
And now we'll get out, too.
Next stop, Houston Astrodome.

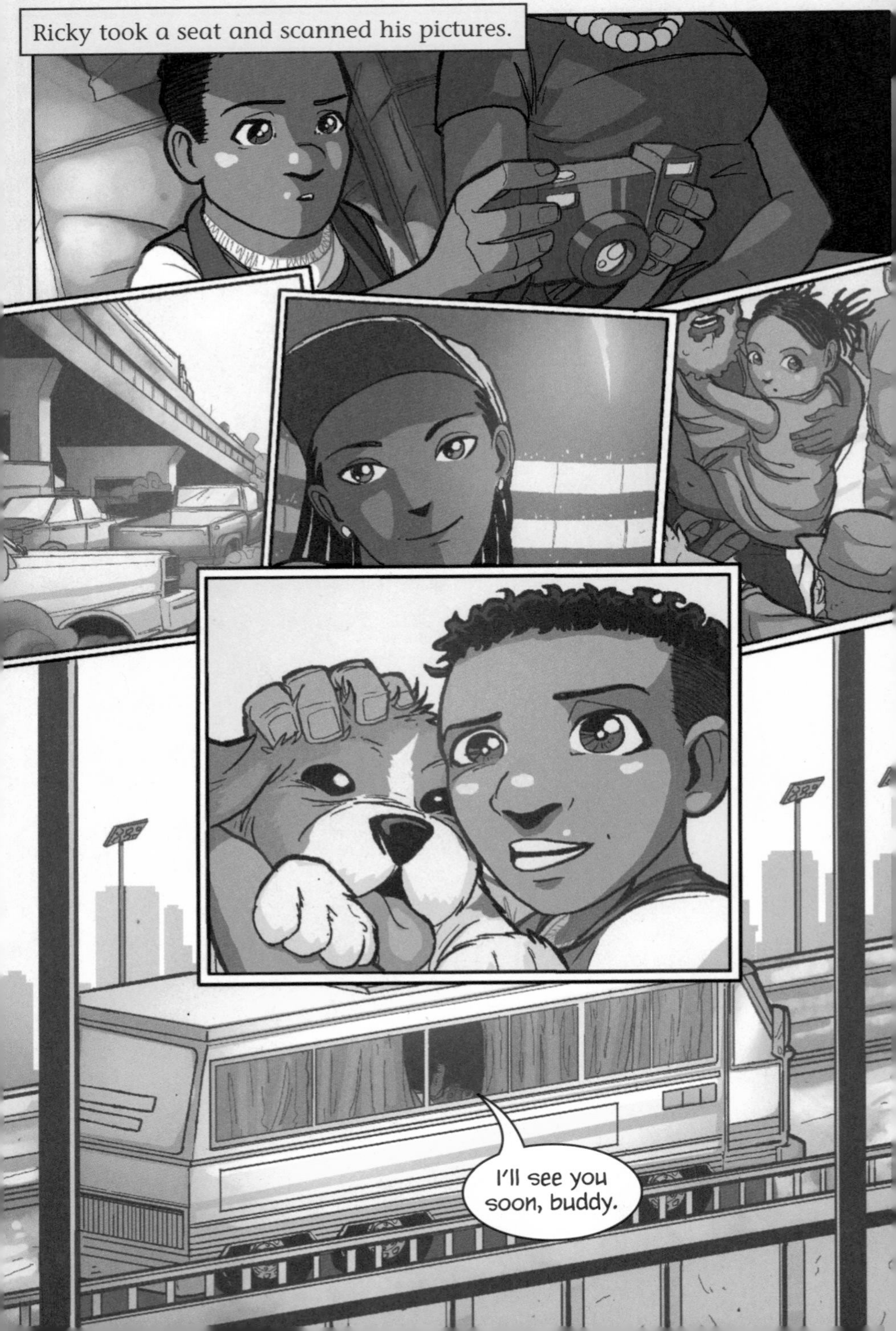
Ricky took a seat and scanned his pictures.
I'll see you soon, buddy.

Then suddenly, the tiny screen went black. The camera's batteries had died. The pictures were still there, of course, trapped on the memory card. But it wouldn't have mattered if they'd been lost. Ricky didn't need them to remember everything he'd been through in the past days.

He gazed out the window at the people waiting for a bus that would take them away. He watched the devastated landscape of New Orleans pass by. No, he didn't need pictures. Hurricane Katrina would be a part of his life for a long, long time.

ABOUT THE AUTHOR

After working more than 10 years as a children's book editor, Stephanie True Peters started writing books herself. She has since written 40 books, including the *New York Times* best seller *A Princess Primer: A Fairy Godmother's Guide to Being a Princess*. When not at her computer, Peters enjoys playing with her two children, hitting the gym, or working on home improvement projects with her patient and supportive husband, Daniel.

ABOUT THE ILLUSTRATOR

Jesus Aburto was born in Monterrey, Mexico, in 1978. He has been a graphic designer, a colorist, and a freelance illustrator. Aburto has colored popular comic book characters for Marvel Comics and DC Comics, such as Wolverine, Ironman, Blade, and Nightwing. In 2008, Aburto joined Protobunker Studio, where he enjoys working as a comic book illustrator.

GLOSSARY

debris (duh-BREE)—scattered pieces of something that has been broken or destroyed

devastated (DEV-uh-stay-tid)—destroyed, or very badly damaged

evacuate (i-VAK-yoo-ate)—move away from an area because it is dangerous there

evacuees (i-VAK-yoo-eez)—people who have been evacuated from a dangerous area

levee (LEV-ee)—a mound of earth or stone built up near a body of water to prevent flooding

makeshift (MAKE-shift)—something made from whatever is available, meant only to be used for a short time

refugee (REF-yooj-ee)—a person who is forced to leave his or her home because of a natural disaster

submerge (suhb-MERJ)—to sink or plunge beneath the surface of water

MORE ABOUT KATRINA

The Superdome is a sports stadium in New Orleans, Louisiana, where professional and college football games are played. In August of 2005, it was used as a "Shelter of Last Resort," according to the New Orleans mayor, for residents of Louisiana and neighboring states during Hurricane Katrina.

Over 9,000 people traveled to the Superdome to ride out the storm. Many went because, rather than leave the state, they had hoped to return home immediately after Katrina had passed. Others were trapped in the area as Katrina approached and were forced to seek shelter at the Superdome. Some evacuees simply had nowhere else to go for shelter. Regardless, more people sought shelter at the Superdome than it could provide for.

The Superdome was not designed to be a shelter, so conditions were very unpleasant. During the storm, two holes ripped in the roof of the Superdome, which allowed water to flood in. Flooding made living conditions even more cramped and uncomfortable. People inside the Superdome had no way to purify water, medical staff wasn't available, toilets didn't work, and food was limited. As survivors from other cities arrived, the number of people inside the Superdome swelled to more than 20,000. Despite these conditions, the Superdome was a far better alternative than being caught outside in the hurricane itself.

On September 1, 2005, 475 buses arrived to evacuate people staying in the Superdome. Evacuees emerged from the Superdome to find their homes destroyed and their city flooded. Most of them were relocated to the Astrodome in Houston, Texas, until they were able to find a permanent place to live.

The evacuees and the hurricane caused major damage to the Superdome. The stadium took one year and $145 million to repair before sports events could take place there again.

DISCUSSION QUESTIONS

1. Hurricanes are among the most dangerous weather conditions for people living along coasts. What type of weather is dangerous in your area?

2. The book says the people in the Superdome grew frustrated. Why? Do you think they received all the help they needed?

3. After Hurricane Katrina, many New Orleans residents left the city for good. Imagine New Orleans was your hometown. Would you want to leave for good or return and start over? Explain.

WRITING PROMPTS

1. Reread the description of the Superdome on page 27. Write your own description of the scene in the form of a poem.

2. Ricky used his camera to record his experience. Imagine he kept a journal instead. Write a journal entry.

3. Write a story about what happens next to Ricky and his family. Will they settle elsewhere or return to New Orleans?

INTERNET SITES

Do you want to know more about subjects related to this book? Or are you interested in learning about other topics? Then check out FactHound, a fun, easy way to find Internet sites.

Our investigative staff has already sniffed out great sites for you!

Here's how to use FactHound:

1. Visit *www.facthound.com*

2. Select your grade level.

3. To learn more about subjects related to this book, type in the book's ISBN number: **9781434211644**.

4. Click the **Fetch It** button.

FactHound will fetch the best Internet sites for you.

3.6/1.0